NOTHING MUCH HAPPENED TODAY

to my daughter, Karen

NOTHING MUCH HAPPENED TODAY

By Mary Blount Christian

Illustrated by Don Madden

Addison-Wesley

Young Scott Books

Text Copyright © 1973 by Mary Blount Christian
Illustrations © 1973 by Don Madden
All Rights Reserved
Addison-Wesley Publishing Company, Inc.
Reading, Massachusetts 01867
Printed in the United States of America
Second Printing
WZ/WZ   01024   10/74

Library of Congress Cataloging in Publication Data

Christian, Mary Blount.
   Nothing much happened today.

   SUMMARY: Three children try to explain to their
mother the chain of events that brought havoc to the
household during her twenty minute absence.
   [1. Humorous stories] I. Madden, Don, 1927–
illus. II. Title.
PZ7.C4528No   [E]   73–4810
ISBN 0–201–01024–0

Mrs. Maeberry held her groceries tightly.
She scurried home to tell her children
about seeing the police chase a robber.

But when she turned down her sidewalk
her mouth flew open.
Soap bubbles—hundreds, thousands, maybe
millions of soap bubbles—were drifting
from her front window.
She ran inside.
"What's happened?" she demanded.
"What's happened here?"
Stephen shrugged. "Nothing much, really."
"But the bubbles!" she yelled.
"Look at those bubbles!"

Stephen shrugged again.
Elizabeth mumbled, "I guess
maybe we did use too many suds
when we bathed Popsicle."
"The dog? You bathed
the dog?" Mother screamed.
"Why did you bathe the dog?"
"He got sugar stuck all over
his fur," Alan, the youngest, said.

Mother set her groceries down.
"I was gone five minutes,
just five minutes. How could Popsicle
get sugar in his fur?"
"He got sugar in his fur
when he knocked over the sugar sack.
That was when he was chasing the cat
through the kitchen," Stephen added.

Mother gasped. "Cat? Cat?
We don't *have* a cat."
"I guess you could say
it was a visiting cat,"
Stephen explained.
"It came through the window."
"The window?" Mother shrieked.
"That cat broke the glass?"
Stephen shook his head.
"Nope. The window was open.
We had to let the smoke out."

Mother grabbed her forehead.
"Smoke! What smoke?"
"The smoke from the oven
when the cake batter
spilled over," Elizabeth volunteered.
Mother waved her arms.
"Why were you baking a cake?"
"For the school bake sale,"
Alan reminded her.
"But," Mother protested.
"But I baked that before
I went to the store."
"We know," Stephen said,
"but that one got ruined."

"Ruined?" Mother repeated.
"How could my beautiful cake
get ruined? I was gone
ten minutes, only ten minutes."
"The cake was knocked onto
the floor, and it's a good
thing it was, too," Elizabeth said.
"I don't understand this.
I don't understand this at all," Mother said.
"It's not so bad," Stephen said.
"We used too many soap suds
on Popsicle because he was covered
with sugar. He knocked the sugar over
chasing the cat.
The cat came through the window
when we let out the smoke.
The smoke is from the spilled cake
batter in the oven.
We were replacing the cake
you baked because that one
got knocked off by the policeman."

Mother's eyebrows shot up.
"Policeman! What policeman?"
"The policeman that ran in
after the robber," Alan told her.

"MY robber?" Mother gasped.
"I—I mean the grocery robber?"
She sank into a chair.
"But tell me, please.
Tell me how a robber
and a policeman ruined my cake."
Stephen smiled. "That's easy.
The robber ran around and around
our kitchen table.
The policeman went
around and around after him.

The policeman accidentally knocked
the cake to the floor.
The robber skidded in the icing.''

Elizabeth interrupted. "And when
the robber fell he hit
his head on Alan's head.
And you know how hard
Alan's head is."
"I know. I know." Mother said.

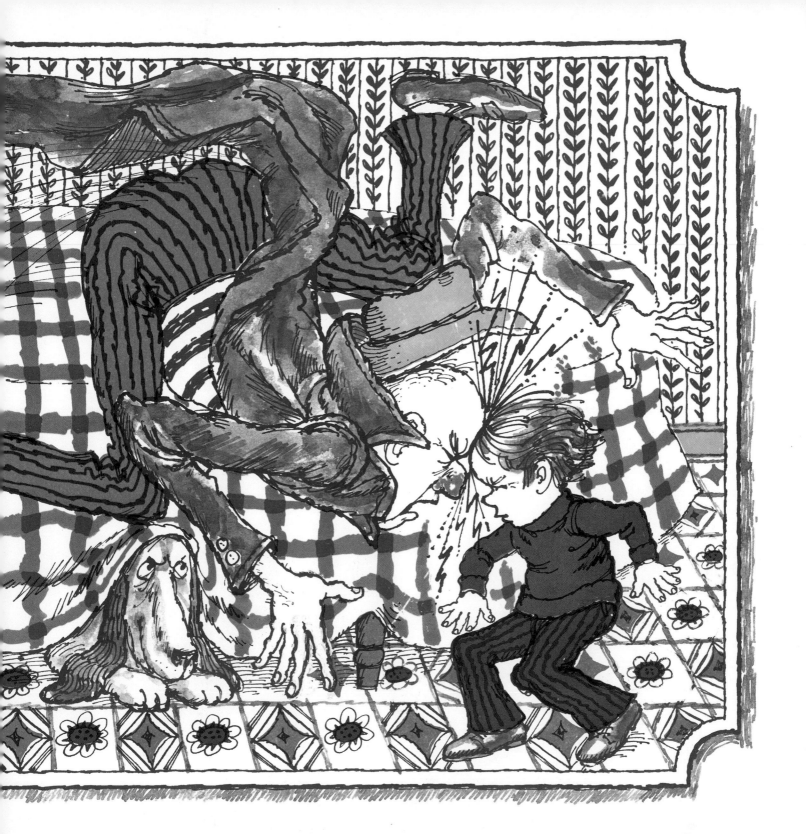

"Let me see now.
The robber ran into here
and the policeman chased him.
They ruined the cake.
When you baked a new one
you made the oven smokey.
Then you opened the window
to let the smoke out
and the cat came in.

Popsicle chased the cat
and knocked the sack of sugar
on himself.
And that's when you bathed him
with too many suds?''

''That's right,'' the three
children said together. ''And that's
when you came home.''
''Twenty minutes at the most,''
Mother said. ''I *know* I couldn't have been gone more
than 20 minutes, anyway.''
''We *told* you
nothing much happened today,''
Stephen said. ''How was your day?''
''Nothing much,'' Mother said,
sliding further back into the chair. ''Nothing much.''

The last soap bubble floated gently
to the end of her nose where it rested,
then popped, and was gone.